"What a lousy idea!"

"Having boys in the gym is stupid!" I blurted out.

"You're wrong, Cindi. I think it will be kind of neat," Darlene said.

It was going to make an awful difference. I knew it. I had grown up around boys all my life. I knew what a pain they could be. I was the only girl in my family, not counting my mom, and believe me, it was more than a drag sometimes. Patrick should have listened to me. I was an expert on boys.

**Look for these and other books
in the GYMNASTS series:**

THE GYMNASTS

#10 BOYS IN THE GYM

Elizabeth Levy

AN
APPLE
PAPERBACK

SCHOLASTIC INC.
New York Toronto London Auckland Sydney

ISBN 0-590-43822-5

12 11 10 9 8 7 6 5 4 3 2 1   0 1 2 3 4 5/9

Printed in the U.S.A.   28
First Scholastic printing, March 1990

To Willie

Can't Keep a Secret

I love secrets, but I have trouble keeping them. Right now I had a secret, and I was bursting to tell somebody. Maybe it has something to do with coming from a big family where everybody is nosy and always wanting to know your business. It's a proven fact that Lauren Baca, my best friend, who's an only child, hates secrets, yet she's good at keeping them. Lauren loves to say that something is a "proven fact." Well, it's a proven fact that I couldn't stop giggling just thinking about my secret.

"Cindi, what are you laughing about?" asked Patrick. Patrick is my coach at the Evergreen Gymnastics Academy. I'm a Pinecone. We're an intermediate group, only some of us are a little more intermediate than others. I don't mean to brag, but I'm probably one of the best of the Pinecones. We don't win many medals at meets; still, I love my team. When we started, Lauren was my only friend who did gymnastics. Now I've got Darlene Broderick and Jodi Sutton, who are my other best friends on the team. The four of us started together, and we think of ourselves as the original Pinecones.

We have two younger teammates. Ti An Truong is only eight — much younger than the rest of us. I like her. She's a little shy.

Ashley Frank can be a real pain in the butt, and she certainly isn't shy. I have to admit that even she isn't all bad. I wouldn't change anything about my team or the Pinecones, even if it meant that we'd win more medals.

When Patrick asked me why I was giggling, I blushed. I could feel my face get red. It's a hazard when you're a redhead like me.

"Look at Cindi," said Ashley. "She looks like a radish."

"You are turning a dangerous pink color," Lauren said.

I giggled again. "Sorry, Patrick, it's just that I've got a secret."

"Uh-oh," said Lauren.

2

"Uh-oh, what?" asked Jodi.

Lauren shook her head. "Cindi's awful at keeping secrets."

"You should never say 'I've got a secret,' " advised Darlene. "It makes everybody want to know what it is. What is it?"

I felt myself turning redder than a fire engine.

"Leave Cindi alone," said Patrick. "If she's got a secret, she doesn't have to tell. But Darlene's right, Cindi. If you want to keep a secret, don't advertise that you have one."

He smiled at me. "You don't look as if it's a serious secret, but if anything's bothering you, you know you can talk to me privately."

"I'm giving a surprise party for Jared," I blurted out. I covered my mouth. Jared is my youngest older brother. I've got four brothers, all older than me. Jared is going to be fourteen. I'm eleven. He's only three years older than me, and he thinks he knows everything. But he didn't know he was getting a surprise party.

"It's not going to be that much of a surprise if you go around telling everybody," warned Darlene. Darlene is thirteen. She's the oldest of the Pinecones, and Jared has a little bit of a crush on her. I don't blame him. Darlene is beautiful. She's the daughter of "Big Beef" Broderick, who plays for the Denver Broncos. I think Darlene thinks that Jared only likes her because she's Big Beef's daughter, but although Jared can be a jerk sometimes, I don't think that's why he likes Darlene.

"Don't you see?" I explained. "The gym is the one place where it's okay to tell about the surprise party. None of his friends are here. No, now I'm safe. It's like having a vaccination. I've told the secret, so I won't tell it to anyone who counts."

"Thanks very much," said Jodi.

"I didn't mean it that way."

"I think we should help you with this party," said Darlene.

"Right," said Lauren. "We can be the 'Cindi Police.' We can put a gag on you every time you're about the spill the beans. I don't buy your vaccination theory. You're going to want to blab it all over the place."

I had to admit Lauren was right.

"Mom and I were going to send out the invitations today," I said. I giggled again.

"You'll probably tell the whole post office," said Lauren.

Patrick shook his head. "Excuse me, Pinecones. Do you think we could stop worrying about Jerry's surprise party and get back to gymnastics?"

"It's *Jared*," said Lauren, laughing at Patrick. "Remember? He's the one who comes to all our meets. He's got glasses and freckles. He's a little goofy-looking."

"He is not," said Darlene.

"And he's got a crush on Darlene," I added.

Patrick held his hands up. "Enough!" he said. "This is a gym, not a gossip center. Let's work on your new beam routine."

"It's too hard," whined Lauren. Beam isn't Lauren's best event. It's not mine, either, but I kind of liked the new routine Patrick was teaching us.

"Cindi, you first," said Patrick.

Our new beam routine had a handstand mount. We used the springboard to jump into the air, reaching for the beam.

I did a fast, low, short hurdle, hitting the board just right. When you hit the board right, it's like having a Slinky on each foot. You fly into the air, and the board gives a satisfying *brong!* sound.

I reached for the beam, grabbing it about six inches from the end and pushed into a handstand.

"Good, Cindi," said Patrick. My hips wobbled a little. The beam is four feet off the ground and only four inches wide. When I'm doing a handstand on the beam, the floor looks like it's a mile away. It's a little scary. I don't mind being upside down on the beam when it's happening fast, but a handstand is such a controlled move.

Patrick put a hand out to steady me.

"Excellent," he said as I took a deep breath. I grinned up at him from my handstand.

"I'll never get that move," said Lauren. I blocked out her voice. I had to concentrate on the rest of the routine. One thing about the beam is that it makes you concentrate. You can't worry about anybody else when you're on it. In fact, that's true of all gymnastic events. Maybe that's why I love gymnastics so much. When you come from a big family like I do, you are always doing things in bunches. In gymnastics, you're part of a team, but you're always alone. When I'm up on the beam, there's nobody else there. It's my world, absolutely. I don't have to worry about anybody else, just about me.

Act Natural

"I definitely think you need help with this party," said Darlene as she pulled on a bright blue jumpsuit. Darlene loves to shop. She's got a whole philosophy built around spreading sunshine to store owners. Someday the Evergreen Mall around the corner from our gym will probably celebrate Darlene Broderick Day, thanking her for all of her business.

"Jared's trying out for the junior high football team this afternoon," I said. "He won't be home till late, so we're going to send the invitations out today. If you guys want to help me put stamps on the invitations that would be great."

"What invitations?" asked Becky.

I clamped my lips together. I may not be good at keeping a secret, but Becky was one person I did not want butting into Jared's party.

Becky Dyson is just plain obnoxious. I hate her. Saddest of all, she's a terrific gymnast. If life were fair, Becky would be worse than the lowest of the Pinecones. Unfortunately, as Patrick has told us, life isn't fair. There are some compensations for Becky being so good, however. She's too good to be a Pinecone. She's in the group above us, the Needles. Noodles is more like it. The only problem is that their group wins all the time. But who cares? I'd rather be a Pinecone.

"It's none of your business," I said. "Some things are secret."

Becky laughed at me. "Well, excuse me. I was just trying to be friendly." I never think of Becky as having feelings that can be hurt. Becky's motto seems to be D.T.A.: Don't Trust Anybody. I guess I forget sometimes that she's human.

Becky turned her back on me. I felt a little bad.

"Can I come help you with the surprise party?" Ti An whispered to me. It was as if she was a little afraid of me after I snapped at Becky. "I can keep secrets."

"Sure," I said, looking at Becky's back as she jammed her gym shoes into her locker. She

8

slammed the door shut and flounced out of the locker room, ponytail swinging.

"What about me?" asked Ashley.

"Can you keep a secret?" I warned her.

Ashley nodded her head. "I promise." This was turning into a farce. We were going to have more people planning the party than going to it.

Lauren caught my eye. She shook her head. "This is what happens when you have a big mouth," she said.

"I tried to keep it secret, honest. And I didn't tell Becky."

"Thank goodness," said Lauren. "You tell *her* about Jared's party, and she'll blab it around town."

"You're right," I said. I slammed my locker shut. "Let's go, Pinecones."

Our dog Cleopatra was waiting for me when the Pinecones turned up the driveway. Cleo's a mutt that we got at the ASPCA. She looks a little like an Airedale with straight hair and a long tail. She jumped all over me as if she hadn't seen me for days. "Down, Cleo," I said. Ti An stood a little bit behind me. "She doesn't bite," I said.

"I know," said Ti An, but she sounded a little bit afraid.

Mom looked surprised when all the Pinecones trooped into our kitchen through the back door.

"It's the surprise-party brigade," said Lauren.

Mom laughed. "Cindi couldn't keep it secret, could she?" Mom asked Lauren.

"I only told the Pinecones," I said.

"We're good at planning parties," said Darlene.

Mom smiled. "I think Jared would have wanted the Pinecones invited, anyhow. He comes to all your meets."

"That's just because of Darlene," said Jodi, digging her elbow into Darlene's side.

Darlene sighed. "Stuff it in a can, Jodi," she said.

Ashley giggled.

Mom got out the invitations. They were great-looking, with the silhouette of a detective all in black and a huge yellow circle with the words *SHHH! It's a Surprise.*

"I think you should tattoo this on Cindi," said Lauren.

"I can keep a secret when I have to," I said defiantly.

Lauren read the inside of the card. "The fifteenth isn't Jared's birthday," she said. "Isn't it on the twentieth?"

"That's part of the surprise," I said. "We figure

Jared would suspect a party on the day of his birthday, but not five days before it."

"Besides, the fifteenth is a day that David has off," said Mom. David is my dad. He's an airline pilot, and he's out of town at least one or two days a week.

"What are you going to do about the RSVP?" Darlene asked Mom. "You can't have kids calling your house. What if Jared picks up the phone?"

"I hadn't thought of that," admitted Mom.

"See?" said Darlene. "I told you that you needed the Pinecones to help."

"You can have them call *our* house," said Lauren. "We've got a machine on all the time, ever since Mom ran for office." Lauren's mom ran for City Council and won.

"Are you sure your mom won't mind?" Mom asked. "I'd better call."

My mom and Lauren's mom have been friends for ages. Mom called Mrs. Baca at her office down at City Hall. She got through right away.

"That takes clout," teased Lauren. I could hear Mom asking Lauren's mom about using the Bacas' phone number. Mom was laughing.

She hung up. "Julia thinks it's a great idea," she said. "She says for the next campaign she needs more boy volunteers, anyhow. Your mom never stops thinking ahead, does she?"

Lauren rolled her eyes. "She keeps threatening to run for mayor," she said.

I wasn't paying much attention. I was looking at the invitation list. "Yuck," I said to Mom. "Do we have to invite Ryan? He'll never keep it secret."

"Ryan is Jared's best friend," said Mom.

"Yeah, but he's twice as obnoxious as Jared," I said. "And Jared's pretty obnoxious."

"This party is *for* your brother," warned Mom. "He's the one who's supposed to have a good time, not us."

"Aha!" I said triumphantly. "You *agree* that Ryan is obnoxious."

"He just loves practical jokes," said Mom. "Remember the time he called a dozen pizza places in town and had them deliver pizza to Jared?"

"Yeah, it was a laugh riot," I said. "The driveway was one big extra-cheese drip. That's what Ryan is . . . one big drip. He's got a laugh like a snort. And he always talks Jared into doing more dumb practical jokes, and I'm always the butt of them. You should have had another kid so I wouldn't have had to be the youngest."

"No, thank you. Five is plenty," said Mom. "Even with Chris and Stephen out of the house, you still eat enough for an army."

"Speaking of food," said Lauren, who's always thinking of food, "what are we going to serve at the party?"

"Pizza," said Mom. "What else?"

"Maybe we should make Cleo come out of the cake!" I said.

"No way. She'll eat it first," said Mom. Cleo loves to eat almost as much as Lauren does.

We were sitting around the kitchen table, just hanging out, laughing, and not really filling out the invitations, all except Ti An, who was carefully printing in the date and the time and the place. Suddenly Ashley looked out the window.

"Does your brother wear glasses?" she asked.

"Yeah," I said. "But don't call him 'Four Eyes.' It makes him mad."

"Does his friend Ryan wear his hair in spikes?" she asked.

"Sometimes. What is this? Are you going to draw his portrait on the invitations?"

"No," said Ashley, "but two boys are walking up your driveway. Your dog is jumping all over the guy with the glasses. But the guy with the glasses doesn't look very happy. He's shooing the dog away."

I ran to the window. "What's *he* doing home? He's supposed to be at football."

"Quick!" said Mom. "Hide the invitations!"

I stuffed them into a pot and put the lid on it.

"Remember where you put them," whispered Darlene. "Don't cook spaghetti in that pot."

"Shhh," I warned her, putting a finger to my lips. "Act natural," I said nervously.

Jodi laughed. "You're the one we've got to worry about," she said.

Unfortunately, I knew she was right.

3

They're Pulling
Your Leg

"Hi, Jared!" I said cheerfully.

Jared looked around the kitchen. "What is this? A Pinecone convention?" he asked.

"I always say the Pinecones are all just nuts," said Ryan with a snort. "What's cooking?" He grabbed for the pot. I took it away and headed for the refrigerator.

"Radish stew," I said. "You'll hate it." Jodi was leaning against the refrigerator. I gestured for her to open it.

Jodi lifted her eyebrows. "Radish stew?" she whispered to me.

"I couldn't think of anything else," I hissed.

"So, Jared," I said, shutting the refrigerator

door behind me. "How did the tryouts go?"

Jared turned thumbs down. "I'm not quick. I'm too small, and the coach said that Ryan and I need upper body work. Guess what he suggested?"

"A body transplant," Ryan snorted.

"Did you get turned down, too?" I asked.

"Naw," said Ryan.

Jared stared at him. "You did, too," he said.

"I didn't really want to be on the team, anyhow. I just tried out because you were doing it. You can't get turned down for something you don't want."

"Well, I wanted to make the team," admitted Jared.

I felt kind of sorry for my brother. At least he admitted that he had wanted something that he didn't get.

"Maybe if you do what the coach said, you can make the team next year," I said. "What did he want you to do? Work out with weights?"

"That's what my dad does," said Darlene.

Ryan sat down next to Darlene. "Your dad is Big Beef Broderick, isn't he?"

Darlene moved her chair away a couple of inches. She hates people who pretend to like her just because she has a dad who is famous.

I scratched my head and looked at Mom. We

had to think of some way to get Jared out of the room so that I could take his invitations out of the refrigerator. People were going to think they were being invited to a party at the North Pole.

Jared sat down on the other side of Darlene. She turned her back on Ryan, making it very clear that she wasn't interested in him. "So, what exactly *did* the coach say to you?" she asked Jared.

"The coach *didn't* suggest just weight work. You aren't going to believe this. . . ."

I was getting mighty impatient. "Come on, Jared, we don't have time for guessing games. If you have something to say, just say it."

Jared ignored me. He drove me crazy. "What are all the Pinecones doing over here, anyhow?" he asked.

"Cooking," said Jodi. "We're cooking up gym stew."

I glared at her.

"It's got a lot of radishes in it." She started to giggle. Ryan gave a half-snort as if he knew what she was laughing about, but he didn't have a clue.

"It's Patrick's recipe," said Jodi. She was practically snorting herself. I could have killed her.

"Is it something you eat to get good at gymnastics?" asked Jared.

Jodi nodded.

"Well, I'm going to need some of that. The coach said that the best way to get in shape would be to get some gymnastics training. He says that there's a new boys' team starting out at a local gym."

I tried to imagine Jared doing gymnastics. He's not really very coordinated, and he doesn't have much upper body strength. The coach was right about that. I'm so strong from all my gymnastics classes I can beat him at arm wrestling. Besides, I didn't think Jared would be good at tumbling. He used to get carsick all the time. On the other hand, Lauren gets carsick and she loves gymnastics.

"Great," I said, faking enthusiasm. "Why don't you call that gym now. Maybe you should find out where it is."

"Oh, that's easy," said Jared. "I know where it is."

"Wonderful," I said. "Go over there right now and sign up."

"That's a good idea," echoed Mom.

"Right," said Darlene. "Gymnastics classes fill up quickly. We should know."

"Do you think Patrick's there now?" Jared asked.

"Very funny," I said.

The rest of the Pinecones were staring at him. "Don't worry," I said. "It's just Jared and Ryan's idea of a joke."

"No, it's not," said Ryan. "The coach told us to go the Evergreen Gymnastics Academy."

I made a face at him. "If you guys think we're going to fall for that, you're dumber than I even thought."

"Maybe it's true," said Ashley. "I think boys in the gym would be cute."

"Ashley, they're just pulling your leg," I said.

Ti An looked down at Ashley's leg. "No, they're not," she said.

Ti An has a tendency to take things a little too literally.

"It's a joke, Ti An," I said with a sigh.

"I'm not joking, Cindi," said Jared. He gave me one of his patented "honest" looks. I'd seen too many of them.

"Yeah, and I've just been asked to quarterback the junior high football team. . . ."

"Will you still have time for gymnastics?" asked Ti An, sounding a little worried.

"That's another joke," I said to Ti An.

"We're not joking," said Ryan, "although personally I think it's a stupid idea. I don't want to jump around in tights walking a stupid plank."

"It's a beam, and boys don't do that," said Darlene. "Gymnastics is great training. Dad sometimes does some of our exercises."

"Darlene, I'm telling you this is just a joke on me that Jared and Ryan are trying to pull. They want me to think that they're really going to Patrick's. Don't encourage them."

Jared stood up. "You know, Darlene, you convinced me. I'm going straight down to the Evergreen Academy and sign up. Come on, Ryan."

"I'm not sure," said Ryan, reluctantly. He was milking this practical joke for all it was worth. "I still think gymnastics is for jerks."

"If that's true, you'll fit in perfectly," I said.

"Is it okay with you, Mom?" Jared asked. "It would mean paying for both Cindi and me to take gymnastics lessons."

"Sure," said Mom. I think she would have agreed with anything in order to get them out of the house.

Finally Jared and Ryan pushed away from the table and went out the back door.

I watched to make sure they got on their bikes and actually went down the driveway.

Mom rescued the invitations from the refrigerator.

"Where do you think they're really going?" Darlene asked.

"Who cares?" I said. "As long as they're out of here."

"I still think it would be a neat idea to have boys in the gym," said Ashley. "I wish it weren't a joke."

"Believe me, it's a joke," I said happily as I stuffed Ryan's invitation into an envelope. "However this is one time that I'm going to have the last laugh. I can't wait to see the look on Jared's face when we pull off this surprise party and he realizes that I kept it secret the whole time."

"Don't get cocky," said Mom. "You've got three weeks to keep it secret. So far, you haven't lasted one day."

"Don't worry, Mrs. Jockett," said Jodi. "The Pinecones can keep a secret, even if Cindi can't."

I grinned happily as I stuffed another envelope. Jared had tried to play a stupid joke on me and he had failed, but I was pulling off a surprise party for him. I was one up and still counting.

4

It's Going to Stink

The next day at practice, Patrick was studying the booklet with the dread yellow cover on it, *The United States Gymnastics Federation Age Group Compulsories for Girls*. It has the compulsory exercises for every level. We're down close to the bottom, Level IVA, but believe me, that's hard enough.

"Patrick's called a meeting of all the groups," said Becky as we came out of the locker room.

"Oh, no, I bet this means we have new compulsories that we're going to have to learn," said Jodi. "I was just getting the hang of the old ones."

"I haven't noticed you getting the hang of anything, Jodi," said Becky. "Maybe hanging onto
bars by your fingernails." She giggled. It came
out more like a snort. Becky reminded me a little
of Ryan.

"Becky, someday I'd like to hang you," said
Jodi.

Becky just laughed. She went across the floor
to join her friends in the more advanced group.
She started to limber up. If only Becky weren't
both strong and limber. She did a graceful backbend and then kicked into a handstand.

Jodi and I watched her. "Why did she think I
was joking when I said I'd like to hang her?" Jodi
asked.

"She's got such a giant ego, I'm surprised
there's room for it in the gym," said Darlene.
"Does anybody know why Patrick wants to meet
with all of us?"

"I don't know," I said. "But I think it's about
new compulsories."

"I had a hard enough time learning the old
ones," complained Darlene.

Patrick put his finger in the book to mark his
place and looked up. He blew his whistle.

"Gather 'round, girls," he said. "I have an announcement to make."

"Please don't tell us we have to learn yet another floor routine," begged Lauren. "Let's call a moratorium on learning new stuff."

Patrick smiled. "Now, Lauren, you can't just stand still. You know my motto."

"Just do it," said Ti An.

"Don't give up," I said.

"Nobody's perfect," said Jodi.

Patrick started laughing. "Okay . . . okay . . . I get it. I have a lot of mottos. But the one I was thinking of is that doing gymnastics is like being a shark — you have to keep moving or you die."

"That's a depressing motto," I pointed out.

"Besides, it's not true," piped up Lauren. "It's a proven fact that scientists now know sharks sleep standing still."

"Maybe we should have a contest to vote on a good motto for Patrick," Jodi joked.

"No, thank you," said Patrick. "I'll stick to my shark motto."

"Are you going to rename us the sharks?" I asked.

Patrick shook his head.

"Maybe that's what he'll call the boys' team," said Ashley. I glared at her to make sure she was joking.

"That's not a bad idea," said Patrick.

Ashley giggled.

Patrick looked around at each of us. "I've called this meeting to announce that the Evergreen Academy *will* be starting a boys' competitive team. I think the Pinecones already know about it."

I gawked at Patrick. "You're kidding!"

"Cindi, I assumed you knew about it because your brother and his friend stopped by late yesterday afternoon and signed up."

"Patrick, cut it out," I wailed. "It's one thing for Jared to tease me, but you're my coach."

"Cindi, I'm not teasing," said Patrick gently. "I was going to make an announcement next week, but I forget what a small world it is around here. Your brother's football coach is a friend of mine — "

"You mean Jared wasn't joking?" asked Darlene in an astonished voice.

"I've been wanting to have a boys' gymnastics team for a long time," said Patrick.

"But boys in the gym is stupid," I blurted out.

"I agree," said Lauren.

"Cindi, Lauren, remember, I was once a boy gymnast."

"But . . . but . . . are you going to be their coach?" My voice was cracking. I couldn't control it.

"No, Jodi's mom will be their coach. She's been

wanting to have a team of her own, and I think she'll be terrific. After all, she was an incredible competitor."

"Mom didn't tell me about this," said Jodi, sounding a little sulky.

"We wanted to keep quiet about it until we were sure we were going to do it," said Patrick.

I still couldn't take it in. Part of me still wanted to believe that Jared had been joking. "Did Jared bribe you to continue this joke?" I begged.

"Cindi, what's the problem? It won't affect the Pinecones."

I felt a surge of relief. "You mean, they won't actually be here?" I asked, sweeping my hand around the gym. "You and Jodi's mom are going to open another gymnastics academy across town?"

"No, no, of course they'll be here. We have plenty of room, and I can't afford to run two places. They won't be working on the same apparatuses as you are, but they'll be working out at the same time. When I built the gym in this old warehouse, I always had in mind having both boys and girls. That's why I wanted such a large space. We'll divide the gym so that they'll have their own workout space."

"I think it's a terrific idea," said Becky. "The

Atomic Amazons have a boys' team." The Atomic Amazons are our rivals in downtown Denver. They've got an incredibly luxurious gym.

"Becky just wants the chance to show off in front of boys," Lauren whispered to me.

"Thank you, Becky," said Patrick, ignoring Lauren and me. "I know that any change is a little unsettling, but I do think it'll be good for the boys to see what great gymnasts we have, and it will be good for your competitive juices."

"But there have *never* been boys here before," I said. "Are you going to have boy Pinecones? It sounds ridiculous."

Patrick looked puzzled. "Cindi, I didn't expect that you'd be so upset. It's not really anything to worry about. It won't make much difference."

"Ha!" I said. "If you believe that, you'll believe anything," I muttered.

Patrick blew his whistle. "Let's break up into our groups and work out. I'd like to see a good workout today from all of you."

"I agree with you, Cindi," muttered Lauren as we lay down on the mats to begin our stretches. "Boys in the gym are going to be more trouble than they're worth."

"What a lousy idea!" I said. I pushed up into a bridge — that's a backbend. "And to think I thought that Jared was kidding," I said, upside down. I felt as if my whole world had been turned upside down.

"I think it'll be kind of neat," said Darlene as she did a bridge next to me.

I collapsed onto my back. "You weren't raised with brothers," I said. "Mark my words, it's going to stink."

"Do you mean literally or figuratively?" Darlene asked.

"Both!" I said.

A Funny Feeling
in My Stomach

"I don't know what I'm supposed to wear," whined Jared.

"Just shorts and a T-shirt," I said. My older brother Tim was waiting to drive Jared and me to Jared's first session at Patrick's gym. We could walk to the gym, but my older brother Tim is sixteen. Sixteen-year-olds love to drive.

Jared was using every stalling tactic in the book. "Just pick any T-shirt, stick it in your gym bag, and let's go," I said. I was getting very annoyed.

"Which T-shirt? Should I wear my Camp Woodmere T-shirt or my Metallica T-shirt? Except for Ryan, I'm going to be meeting a bunch of strangers."

"What difference does it make?" I asked him.

"Come on, Cindi," said Tim. "I remember the first day I drove you and Lauren to the Evergreen Gymnastics Academy. You were so nervous you almost threw up."

"That was Lauren, not me. I never get carsick."

"Please," begged Tim, giving Jared a worried look. "Don't give him any ideas."

"You know, Jared, you have to do a lot of somersaults in gymnastics," I teased. "A lot of turning upside down."

Jared was starting to look a little green. He stuck his camp T-shirt in his gym bag and hurried out the door.

"Cindi, you're a grade-A troublemaker," said Tim.

"Thank you," I said, taking it as a compliment. Tim drove over to Lauren's house to pick her up. She was standing outside of her town house, all ready.

"Hi ya, Jared," she said cheerfully. "You ready for your first day?"

Jared grunted. I thought it was kind of cute that he was so jittery.

Lauren kept prattling on. "I remember my first day, when we got inside and Patrick said we had to be tested; I thought I was gonna die."

"Testing!" squawked Jared. "What testing?"

"Oh, nothing too hard," I said, winking at Lauren. "You have to swing from the bars, do a double-back. . . . Probably, being a guy, you'll have to do the iron cross on the ring. . . . Let's see. . . ."

Jared was looking a little sickly. "I don't even know what those things mean. It's like going to a foreign country without a dictionary." Jared began to bite on his thumbnail. He used to bite all his nails, but lately he's been trying to stop. He saves one thumbnail for nibbling on, and he only does that when he's really nervous.

"Jared," said Lauren, "Cindi's teasing you. The testing isn't so hard."

We pulled up in front of Ryan's house. Tim honked the horn, but nothing even stirred in the house. I looked at my watch. "Patrick doesn't like it when we're late," I complained. "Why couldn't he be on time?"

"Stop complaining," said Jared.

"Are we going to have to go together all the time?" I said. "Because if so, you'd better tell Ryan that he has to be on time."

"Lighten up, Cindi," warned Tim. "We're still early. You'll be there in plenty of time."

Just then Ryan came barreling out of his town

house. Ryan was wearing a bright green Hawaiian shirt that I thought was hideous. He probably thought it was cool.

"Why were you late?" I asked him. "Were you deciding what to wear, like Jared? If so, you should go back and change."

"I was deciding whether or not to come," said Ryan, settling down in the backseat next to me. "I think gymnastics is a lousy idea. I don't care how good that coach is. I hear he was a star on the University of Colorado team . . . but who cares? It's not as if he went to the Olympics or anything."

"That's Patrick," I explained. "Sarah Sutton, Jodi's mom, is the one who'll be coaching you."

Ryan turned and frowned at me. "A woman?" he exclaimed. His voice cracked. Ryan's and Jared's voices were both changing. They sounded like they had colds most of the time, except when their voices cracked into a squeak. Teenage boys sound extremely funny, like cartoon characters.

"A woman," I mocked Ryan, "who just happens to be one of the best gymnasts in the world. She comes from St. Louis, and she was on the senior national team. She was once one of the top gymnasts in the country."

"I didn't know that," said Jared. "Jodi's mom, huh? She sounds kind of neat."

"She is," I said.

"She's a woman," repeated Ryan.

"Gosh, Ryan, you are so smart," I said sarcastically. "You figured that out all by yourself. If she's Jodi's mother, she must be a woman. I bet you did great on your biology test."

"This isn't funny, Cindi," muttered Ryan. "I don't like this."

Jared gave me a funny look, as if begging me not to say anything more. But honestly, Ryan was being such a dinosaur. Even Tim was trying hard not to laugh.

"Welcome to the end of the twentieth century," said Tim. "Look, Jodi's mom sounds like she really knows what she's doing."

"Easy for you to say," snapped Ryan. "You play football. Nobody makes fun of you."

"And at high school our fitness coach is a woman. She's in the weight room with us. She can bench press twice her own weight."

Ryan huddled in the corner of the car and chewed on his fingernail. No wonder he and Jared were best friends.

We pulled onto the road behind the Evergreen Mall. It's paved, but that's about all you can say for it. It's got huge potholes from winter storms, and it's never fixed up, because the only things on this road are a couple of abandoned gasoline tanks and Patrick's gym.

"I don't know about this," said Ryan. "How did I let you talk me into it?"

Lauren laughed. "You sound just like me."

"Shut up, pipsqueak," muttered Ryan.

"He's just nervous," Jared whispered to Lauren.

We got out of the car. Darlene was just pulling up with her dad.

"There's Big Beef," said Jared, poking Ryan in the arm. "I told you we'd meet him if you took gymnastics."

Darlene's dad rolled down his window and gave Lauren and me a big smile. "Afternoon, tigers," he said.

"It's not tigers . . . it's Pinecones," I teased him back. I really like Big Beef. He may be huge and a celebrity, but he's about the nicest dad in the world. He's always got compliments for us. I think he genuinely likes me.

"The Pinecones *are* tigers," said Big Beef. Darlene stepped out of the sports car.

"Hi, Jared," she said, waving at him. "Welcome to the Evergreen Gymnastics Academy." She gave him a mock bow of welcome.

Jared bowed back. "Pleased to be here," he said.

Ryan punched him in the back. "You sound like a toady," he whispered to Jared.

"Shut up," said Jared cheerfully. I was glad to hear him tell Ryan to shut up.

Jared went over to Big Beef's car. He introduced Ryan, who got that stupid look people sometimes get on their faces when they're around celebrities. It was as if Big Beef were the only person in the universe.

"So Patrick's finally got guys in the gym," said Big Beef.

"We're only doing it so that we can make the football team next year, sir," said Ryan.

"Some of that stuff looks mighty scary. At least in football we *try* to keep both feet on the ground," said Big Beef.

"Football isn't for wimps, though," said Ryan, trying to sound respectful. I thought he sounded like a dork.

"Neither is gymnastics," said Big Beef. " 'Bye, honey." Darlene leaned through the window and gave him a kiss. "Go get 'em, Pinecones," said Big Beef as he drove off.

"I wish I'd had my camera," muttered Ryan. "I could have had my picture taken with Big Beef."

"He hangs out here all the time," said Jared.

"Ryan's an idiot," I whispered to Darlene. "I think the only reason he's coming to gymnastics is to meet your dad."

"He's probably just nervous," Darlene whispered back. "I remember my first day. I was so tense I could hardly walk through the door."

"Yoo-hoo!" shouted Becky, as her mother dropped her off. "Hi, everybody!"

"Speaking of somebody who should never have been let in the door," I said.

"I wonder why she's being so friendly," asked Lauren. "What's she up to?"

Ryan turned around. "Who's that?" he asked me. "She's pretty."

Becky has blonde hair and sneaky blue eyes. She's got long legs and a short torso. Jodi once described her as a buzzard walking on tiptoe. Ryan would go for the buzzard type.

"Hi, Cindi," said Becky with a big smile. Becky never gives me a smile. "Is this your brother?" She stuck out her hand to Ryan. Becky knows who my brother is. She's seen him at meets. She's even met him at a party at Darlene's. But Jared's not as good-looking as Ryan.

"No," I said, "this is Ryan. He's trying out for the team. Becky's one of our best gymnasts."

"Why, thank you, Cindi," said Becky. She put

her arm around me. It felt like it weighed a ton.

"Cindi doesn't usually give me compliments," she said.

Ryan grinned at Becky. "I don't know what I'm doing here," he said. "I don't know a thing about gymnastics."

"Oh, it's easy to pick up," said Becky. "Really, it just seems to come naturally to some people."

I rolled my eyes toward the sky. Becky's been taking gymnastics intensely for about six years. She works twice as hard as anyone. Why did she have to lie about it, and pretend it all came naturally?

Jared squared his shoulders. "I guess we have to go in, huh?" he said.

I looked up at the Evergreen sign above the door. I could remember my first day going through the door and how nervous I was. Then I thought about how much I loved the place.

"Come on, Jared," I said, opening the door for him.

I watched my brother's back as he went in. Lauren slipped in beside me.

"I was just thinking about our first day," she whispered to me.

"You know, I was scared that day, too," I admitted.

Lauren stared at me. "You?" she exclaimed. "You're the one who always wants to try out something new."

I shook my head, shocked that that was how Lauren saw me.

"Not me," I said.

"I don't believe you," said Lauren. "You're the one who's never scared of something new."

I shrugged my shoulders. Even my best friend didn't believe me when I told her that I had been scared.

I had a funny feeling in my stomach now. Everybody thought I was just joking about not wanting boys in the gym, about not wanting things to change, but I loved Patrick's just the way it was.

I loved it because it was the one place in my life where I could get away from boys, not just from my brothers, but from the silly ways that girls get when there are boys around.

I was going to hate having boys in the gym. I just knew it.

6

I'm an Expert on Boys

Besides Jared and Ryan, there were about five other boys standing around inside the gym, and they all looked uncomfortable. I didn't know any of the others. Most of them looked around twelve or thirteen. There were a couple of guys who looked like they had done some gymnastics already. Gymnasts look different than other athletes. They've got strong upper bodies, but they don't bulk up the way football players do. A couple looked really young, even younger than me.

Jodi, Ti An, and Ashley were standing in a corner, looking them over. Jodi waved at Jared.

He gave her a weak wave back. "Jared's so nervous he almost got sick in the car coming over here," I said.

"Poor guy," said Darlene.

"Look at them all," whispered Jodi. "They *all* look nervous."

"I think that blond is so cute," said Ashley.

I shifted around uneasily. On a normal day, we'd just come in, go to the locker room, and get to work. Here we were standing around as if the boys were movie stars.

"Locker room," I said out loud. "Where are they going to change?"

Nobody paid any attention to me. They were too busy staring at the boys.

"Which blond?" asked Jodi.

Ashley pointed to Ryan. "He's Jared's friend," said Lauren. "He's the one Cindi doesn't like, but I think he's funny."

"Wait till you get to know him," I said.

Just then Patrick came out of his office with Jodi's mom. He went up to the group of boys and shook each of their hands. Jared didn't even look up when Patrick shook his hand. He kept his eyes on his feet as if they were about to do something embarrassing. I was embarrassed for him.

Patrick blew on his whistle.

"I want to welcome our new gymnasts," he said. "Some of you have had some training; some of you are just beginning. You'll find that gymnastics never stops challenging you."

"I wish it were a little less challenging," whispered Lauren.

Luckily Patrick didn't hear her. "Your new coach will be Sarah Sutton. She was on our national team when she used to compete. It's an honor to have her here in Denver. I know how much she loves to teach and to win."

Jodi shifted her weight uneasily behind me. "Those poor suckers don't know what they're in for," she said. "Mom will work their butts off."

"Shh," I warned her.

Patrick turned around toward us. "I know that my girls' teams join me in welcoming our new boys' team and wishing you well. Let's get started. Girls, it's time to get changed and start warming up."

"Where are the boys going to change?" I asked.

Ashley snickered as if I had just said something outrageous, but it seemed like a reasonable question to me.

"We'll temporarily be using the parents' lounge as a boys' locker room," said Patrick. "Soon I'll build a new addition with locker rooms and showers for the boys, but for now they'll have to use the parents' lounge. It has a sink, and I'm going to be able to install temporary showers. It'll be a little rough, but I hope you guys won't mind."

"Rough?" I exclaimed. "It's got the ice machine and the refrigerator and all those comfortable couches."

"All right!" said Ryan. "I like the idea of our own ice machine."

"Why can't we use the parents' lounge, and they can have our locker room?" I said.

Patrick scowled at me. "Cindi, it's the parents who will be inconvenienced."

"And where are *they* going to sit?" I asked. "They're going to hate it." The parents' lounge was the greatest place in the whole gym. It was separate from the gym because Patrick didn't like parents making us nervous.

But not many parents came to watch every day, and the parents' lounge was the one quiet place where we could always go talk to Patrick.

His office was just a cramped little space on the second floor, and it felt too much like talking to a teacher having to go up to Patrick's office.

And what about ice! We were always injuring ourselves and having to put ice on our injuries. What were we going to do now?

"I'm setting up a temporary lounge on the second floor by my office."

"But then there will no place we can go to talk to you privately. Where are you going to go?"

"Cindi, I'm running this gym, remember?"

I blushed. "Sorry."

Darlene grabbed my arm. "It's not such a big deal," she warned me. "Don't make a federal case out of it. At least we still have our locker room."

"It just doesn't seem right."

"It's time for gymnastics, boys and girls," said Patrick.

"Boys and girls," I muttered under my breath. Why, even Patrick didn't put girls first! And he said nothing was really going to change.

Patrick was just fooling himself if he thought he could introduce boys into the gym without it making a big difference!

It was going to make an awful difference. I knew it. I had grown up around boys all my life. I knew what a pain they could be. I was the only girl in my family, not counting my mom, and believe me, it was more than a drag sometimes. Patrick should have listened to me. I was an expert on boys.

7

Another Bombshell

I had been right. The first few days seemed like a disaster to me. All the girls were distracted. The boys made a lot of noise, particularly Ryan with his obnoxious, nervous snort that seemed to ring from the rafters.

I was hoping Patrick would decide after one week that the experiment with a boys' team was a mistake. The stores in the mall probably loved it. Some of the girls were coming in with a new outfit every day. Becky was the most obvious.

On the following Monday she had on a brand-new unitard, a one-piece leotard with legs that was incredibly flashy, with bold blue and white stripes with red stars across the top.

"She looks like one of those giant flags in front of car lots," said Jodi.

"I bet she wore that just so the boys could see her," said Darlene.

I had to laugh. "Darlene, I haven't seen your leotard before," I said. Darlene was wearing a purple iridescent leotard.

"Oh, this old thing," pooh-poohed Darlene. "I've had this for ages."

"Darlene," I said.

She giggled. "Okay, okay, I've had it for a while, but this is the first time I've worn it. It was sitting in my drawer. But it's not as garish as Becky's, is it?"

"No," I reassured Darlene, but I was getting tired of all the talk about fashion.

Jared and Ryan and a couple of the other boys came out chatting from their locker room, which I, for one, continued to call the parents' lounge. The boys were supposed to go to their side of the room, but Ryan stopped at the beam. "Is this where I get to walk the plank?" asked Ryan. He put his hands on one of the beams.

"It's not as easy as it looks," I said.

Ryan laughed at me. "When I was a little kid, I used to walk on the top of the roof of my garage. It was much higher than this."

Ryan tried to swing his leg over the beam, but

I don't think he realized that four feet five inches is higher than it looks. He got hung up with one knee over the beam but no leverage to pull himself up.

"What's the matter? Need a push?" I asked. I got behind and shoveled Ryan up onto the beam. Ryan clung there with one leg on each side.

"*We* stand up on it," I said.

"We even do cartwheels on it," said Lauren. She hopped up on the opposite beam and did a perfect split. I grinned at her.

Ryan was staring at her, still afraid to even stand up on the beam.

Luckily for him, he got in trouble before he could even try. Jodi's mother blew her whistle.

"You!" she shouted. "Off the beam. Nobody gets on *any* apparatus until I tell you to and until you warm up properly. You can hurt yourself. You should have at least learned that in your first week."

Ryan blushed. "She's a drill sergeant," he said as he slunk off the beam.

"Don't worry," bragged Jared, trying to cheer up his friend. "The beam just looks pretty. It can't be hard. Not like the rings that *we* have to use."

Becky simperingly agreed. "I love to watch you

boys on the rings," she said. "It takes so much strength."

" 'So much strength,' " I mocked her. "Becky, you're stronger than these guys, any day. I can beat them at arm wrestling, and I'm not as strong as you are."

"Oh, Cindi, you're so silly," said Becky, giggling.

I made a face and walked away. Becky was disgusting enough when she just had an ego problem. "When she puts on that cutesy 'I'm so weak' act for the guys, I want to puke," I whispered to Darlene.

"I think it's kind of funny to see her act so stupid."

"She's not the only one acting stupid," I said.

Darlene gave me a funny look. "*I* don't act that way," she said, sounding insulted.

"I know," I admitted. "It's just that Becky's stronger than Jared *or* Ryan any day."

"Don't worry about it," said Darlene. She smiled at Jared, who smiled back.

Just then Patrick came out of the back of the gym, pulling a handcart with a pile of what looked like new equipment behind him.

"What do you think that is?" I asked.

"Maybe we're finally getting a foam pit," I said.

Some of the gymnastic clubs had foam pits so that you could practice double-backs and complicated release moves from the bars without always needing a spot. Patrick had once said that we'd get a foam pit eventually.

He blew his whistle.

"Sarah and I have decided that we're going to put up temporary screens," he said. "It'll divide the girls' area of workout from the boys'. We could use a little help."

"I thought you said there'd be no difference when we had boys," I grumbled.

"Cindi," said Patrick, "we've just had one week with boys. Stop complaining."

I shut my mouth. I didn't want Patrick to think of me as a complainer. "Sorry," I said quietly. "I'll help."

"Thanks," said Patrick. "I've put tape down where the screens should go."

"It's right where we normally do our floor work," I blurted out.

Patrick pointed to the corner of the room where he had moved our floor mats. "We have plenty of space over there," he said.

"You're right," I said quickly. I grabbed one of the screens to show Patrick I was a good sport. They were heavy. I grunted as I lugged it over to the middle of the floor where Patrick had placed the tape.

"Here, I'll take that," said Ryan.

"It's okay," I panted. "I've got it." I took a few steps forward toward the tape. The screen felt like it weighed a hundred pounds. I'm sure it didn't, but it was darned heavy and awkward to carry.

"No, no, let me take it," insisted Ryan. "It's too heavy for a girl." I felt like bopping Ryan on the head with the screen.

Behind me, I could hear Becky tittering. I knew Ryan was just trying to make a macho impression on her.

"Too heavy for a girl." I couldn't believe the jerk had actually said that.

"Okay, strong man," I said. "You carry it. Boys are built for heavy labor." I handed the screen over to Ryan.

He staggered under its weight, tottered around, and finally had to put it down. He was breathing hard.

"What's the matter, Ryan?" I asked. "Is it a little heavy for you?"

Ryan stared at the screen. "How come you could lift it?" he asked.

"I've been taking gymnastics for a long time,

sonny," I said. I picked up the screen, trying to make it look as if it didn't weigh a thing. I was sweating, but I lifted it without grunting and put it on top of my head. Actually it was a lot easier to carry that way than by using just my arms, but Ryan didn't know that.

Ryan went back to the pile, and *together* he and Jared carried one of the screens to the middle of the floor.

"It takes two boys to do what it takes one girl to do," I said as I passed them going back for another screen. Becky was coming toward me carrying one of the screens with no trouble. "But, of course, boys are so much stronger. Right, Becky?"

Becky pretended not to hear me. Lauren and Jodi were carrying one of the screens together. "That's a sissy *boy's* way of doing it," I said as I passed them.

"Stop goading them," said Lauren. I glared at her.

I went back for another screen, but they were already all gone.

"With everyone working together, that went very smoothly," said Patrick. He looked at the gym as if he were pleased. The screens were made out of opaque plastic squares, but they were old, and some of the plastic had holes in it, the size of portholes that you could see through. The screens looked dwarfed by the high ceilings in the gym. They didn't fit tightly together, so every few feet there were a few inches that you could look through.

"It's not exactly a brick wall," I said to Patrick. "The boys will be able to see us."

"And vice versa," said Ryan.

"The screens are more of a psychological barrier than a physical one," said Patrick. "I don't have any objection to the two groups watching each other a little. It was getting to be too big of a distraction."

"It's ugly," said Lauren.

"I couldn't agree with you more," I said, glad that Lauren had said it first and not me. "Where did you get them, Patrick, at a fire sale?" I asked.

"Actually, they were left over in the basement right here. I think the factory used them to divide areas once. I always knew I had a reason for not throwing them out."

"They look really yukky," I said. "They make the gym look all cut up. I loved it when it was open."

"Cindi," asked Patrick, "could you try opening your mouth without complaining about the changes in the gym for a little while?"

I hung my head a little. "Sorry," I said.

Patrick put his arm around my shoulders. "Me, too. Maybe I was a little harsh. Let's go work out," he said. "Besides, I've got something to tell the Pinecones that will take their minds off boys in the gym."

"What's that?" I asked.

"I think I'd better tell all the Pinecones together," he said.

If Patrick thought he was cheering me up with those words, he was wrong. He had already dropped one bombshell on us. We didn't need another one.

If It Was Easy, Everybody Would Do It

Patrick told us to sit on the mats surrounding the beam. He carried the yellow book of compulsory exercises in one hand and the green book of points in the other.

"Don't tell me," groaned Darlene. "We've got another competition set up that we don't know about."

"Probably with the Atomic Amazons," said Ti An. "It's just our luck."

"I wonder when the Pinecones are going to let me finish a sentence," said Patrick. "Since you all seem to think you know what I'm going to say before I say it, maybe I shouldn't even bother telling you what I had in mind."

"Sorry, Patrick," said Darlene quickly. "I guess I should have waited to hear what you had to say."

"It's not really her fault," I said, wanting to come to Darlene's rescue. "We've had so many changes lately that we don't want any more."

"Cindi, will *you* let me finish what I started to say?" asked Patrick.

I could feel myself turning radish color again. I shut my mouth.

Darlene smiled at me.

Patrick put the books down on the beam and placed his hands behind him. Effortlessly he pushed down on his arms and swung up onto the beam. Using only his arms for support, he held himself above the beam and then slowly lowered his seat onto the beam.

"Looks easy, doesn't it?" he asked. "It's called a reverse press."

"Not exactly," I said. "It takes a lot of strength, I bet."

"You're right, Cindi. It's a strength move, but I've been impressed with the Pinecones' conditioning. In fact, I've been impressed with the Pinecones' overall progress lately. I want to test to see if most of you are ready for the next level. The test will be quite simple — just two moves that will indicate your skills. I don't want you to get all nervous about being tested on too many things — just the handstand on the beam and then the reverse press. I want you to hold the press for fifteen seconds. You've already learned the handstand mount."

Patrick leaned over on the beam and pulled out his calendar. "We'll have the test on the fifteenth of the month."

"That's the day of — " I almost blurted out "Jared's birthday party."

Lauren and Jodi both made a dive for me and clapped their hands over my mouth.

"Idiot," whispered Lauren. "Remember, he's here now."

"Girls," said Patrick, sounding a little annoyed, "would you please leave Cindi alone!"

"They were just doing it for my own good," I admitted. "I don't see why we need this test, Patrick. Ordinarily we all just learn a new routine at our own pace."

"Cindi," said Patrick, "I have no doubt that you'll learn the routine and pass the test in flying colors. In fact, why don't you be the first one to try it?"

"I'm the guinea pig, huh?" I whispered to Lauren as I got off the floor.

"You're the only one who Patrick thinks can do it," Lauren whispered back.

I picked my way around Ti An and Ashley to the front of the group. Patrick put the springboard at a right angle to the center of the beam. He stood at the side of the board next to the beam, ready to steady me as I tried the handstand.

"Try to take a full run so that you can get good height for your drive off the board," said Patrick.

"What if I dive straight over the beam?" I asked.

"I'm standing here to stop you," he said. "Go for it."

I smiled at him. "I like that motto much better than the one about the shark," I said.

Patrick laughed. "Quit stalling, Cindi."

I walked back to the new dividing screen. "I can't take *that* long a run anymore," I yelled to Patrick.

"Cindi," he said, "you don't need a hundred-yard dash. You've got plenty of room."

I saw Jared peering out at me from between the screens. He made me nervous. "Go away," I hissed at him.

"Jared," said Jodi's mom. "It's your turn to try the rings."

Jared's face disappeared from the screens.

I started my run for the beam.

"Stop, Cindi," said Patrick. "Where's your salute?"

"I forgot," I admitted. When we're in competition we have to salute the judges before every event. Patrick wants us to get in the habit of doing it without thinking, but my mind was really messed up today.

Doing a running mount on the beam is hard because, unlike the vault, you're not trying to get over something. You have to stop your momentum and try to stay on the beam.

I ran with my elbows close to my body, looking straight ahead. I tried to run on the balls of my feet, not on my tiptoes. I get a lot more control and strength from the balls of my feet. I hit the board and jumped for the beam, reaching out for the beam with my arms straight.

Patrick steadied me as I pushed into a handstand on the beam.

"Good, Cindi." Patrick had a heavy hand on my hips because I was teetering all over the place.

Patrick guided me with his voice. "Open your legs, and slowly come down from the handstand, keeping your weight on your hands. Keep your chest and head up high."

Sweat was dripping down from my face. This move depended on brute strength. I didn't think I had enough, but I managed to press down with Patrick taking most of the weight off my hands.

"Great, Cindi," said Patrick. "That's enough." He helped me down.

"That's hard!" I exclaimed, looking back at the beam.

Patrick grinned at me. "If it was easy, everybody could do it. That's why it's going to be the test."

I turned to go, and then I stopped. Something was bothering me. "Patrick," I asked, "what exactly do you mean by test?"

Patrick looked puzzled. "A test. Come on, Cindi. You've had tests before."

"Yeah, but in school, it's pass or fail. In gymnastics, even if we don't do a trick, we keep on trying."

"Exactly," said Patrick. "That's what makes gymnastics so great."

I was dripping sweat.

"Cindi's right," said Lauren. "We were tested when we began. Why don't you test the boys?"

The other Pinecones started laughing. "Yeah, test the boys! Test the boys!" chanted Jodi. Ti An and Ashley chimed in.

Patrick held up his hands for us to keep quiet.

"Enough's enough. Lauren, it's your turn."

As I watched Lauren struggle and fail to do the new move, I realized that Patrick had never answered my question. We had all gotten too distracted by chanting "test the boys." It was still another reason I didn't like boys in the gym.

9

A Lousy Feeling

All that week, as we concentrated on learning the reverse press, I thought about Patrick's words about the test, and I still didn't get it. He had said he wanted to see if "most" of us were ready for the next level. What if some of the Pinecones didn't pass? Would Patrick split up the Pinecones? The very idea of splitting up the Pinecones seemed too scary even to think about . . . but Patrick *had* said "most of you." He hadn't said "all of you."

I watched more carefully than I could ever remember watching as the other Pinecones got up to try the move.

Jodi went next. Jodi's rarely afraid of any-

60

thing. In fact, she's got more courage than skills. She flew off the board, and even with Patrick trying to hold her into a handstand, she tumbled down onto the mats on the other side.

"Whoops!" said Jodi. "I guess I went a little too far."

"The secret of this move is tight control," said Patrick. "You have to think 'control' from the minute your arms reach out for the beam."

"I've never been much for control," admitted Jodi.

"You're going to be able to get it," said Patrick. "Come back here, and try it without the run. I'll hold you."

Patrick steadied Jodi as she did a handstand onto the beam. She wobbled a little, but her legs were pretty straight. Then he helped her go into a straddle and gently lower her legs so that she was perched above the beam in a press.

"Good, Jodi," said Patrick. "I think you understand the mechanics now."

Jodi grinned at him. "I'm going to get it," she said confidently.

Patrick patted her on the back. "Now, that's the attitude I like."

Ti An tried it next. It was extraordinary. Ti An is so tiny. She doesn't look very muscular, but she's got amazing upper body strength. She was able to hold herself over the beam in the reverse press for nearly thirty seconds.

"Bravo!" shouted Patrick.

Ashley didn't do as well as Ti An, but she did it pretty well. Darlene was scared of the mount. She's tall, and sometimes it's hard for her to control her legs. She managed to hold her handstand. She needed an even heavier spot than I did, but she managed okay.

"I'll never do it," muttered Lauren as we both watched Darlene lower her hips for the reverse press.

"Sure you will," I said. "Patrick really does most of the work."

Lauren just looked at me. "You're just saying that to make me feel better. I can't do the reverse press."

"You've got lots of strength. And the handstand's like a vault. You're a great vaulter."

"I like vaulting 'cause it's quick. You're not supposed to stay on the horse. I can't even do the first part of this move, much less the reverse press. I'll never get it."

"Quit being so negative," I warned Lauren.

"I'm just being honest," she said as Patrick called her up to the beam.

"Don't be honest. Be positive," I shouted to her.

Lauren made a face. "I think that ranks with Patrick's shark motto," she grumbled at me.

Lauren went back practically to the screen to begin her run. I had a feeling she was going too far. She ran flat-footed, almost tentatively. I knew she wasn't going to make it from the way the board sounded when she landed on it.

She fell to her knees even before she reached out for the handstand on the beam.

Patrick helped her up. "Lauren, the idea is to use the board to get over the beam, not under it," he said, smiling. "Don't worry. You'll get it." Patrick looked at his watch. "It's been a long afternoon," he said. "I think everybody's got the concept of this new move. Let's move on to some tumbling on the mats while you've still got a little strength."

Lauren bit at the cuticle around her thumbnail. She looked up at Patrick. "Wait a minute," she said. "What happens if I flunk the test?"

"Lauren, it's just the first week of learning this new trick. I don't want you thinking so negatively."

"See, that's what I said," I whispered in Lauren's ear. She just sighed. Patrick moved up to where the mats were set up for our floor exercise.

I got to Lauren's side again as quickly as I could. I didn't want her feeling bad.

"Patrick's right, you know. The first week of learning a new trick is always the hardest," I said.

Lauren didn't look up. She chewed on her thumb. "Cindi, quit trying to cheer me up, okay?" she asked.

I didn't know what to do, so I shut up. I guess sometimes shutting up is the best thing you can do for a friend, but it was a lousy feeling.

Remember the Shark

We went into the locker room. I tore off my leotard and put on my T-shirt and jeans. "Aren't you going to shower and wash your hair?" asked Becky.

"I never wash my hair here at the gym," I said. "It takes too long to dry." I sniffed under my armpits. "Not too bad," I said.

"That's so disgusting," said Becky.

"Come off it. It's no different than I've ever been."

"I know," said Becky. "But now that there are boys in the gym, you shouldn't be so revolting." Becky stepped into the shower.

"There're some kinds of dirt that you can't wash off," I said to Lauren.

Lauren laughed halfheartedly. "I wish Patrick hadn't scheduled the test on the same day as your party for Jared."

"What's the difference?" said Darlene. "It'll be a double celebration."

"Ha!" grunted Lauren. "What'll we have to celebrate?"

"I agree," I said. "Some celebration. Now I suppose I'll have to invite all those boys on Jared's team. At least some of them don't look as bad as Ryan."

"Stop worrying about Ryan," said Jodi. "I think he's kind of cute."

"All he does is joke around," I complained.

"What's wrong with that?" joked Jodi.

I laughed. It was true that Jodi liked to joke around as much as Ryan.

"Isn't it amazing?" I mused. "How people you like can do something and it never bothers you, but if you don't like somebody it always bothers you."

"More wisdom from the great philosopher," grumbled Lauren as she put her gym shoes in her bag.

"Come on, Grumpy." I tried to kid Lauren. "Life isn't so bad."

"How would you feel if you were going to be the one Pinecone to be left behind?"

"Lauren, Patrick won't split up the Pinecones," said Jodi.

"Jodi's right," I echoed, but I had been worried about the same thing myself. I just hadn't had the nerve to say it out loud.

"You guys don't listen," said Lauren, practically in tears. "Patrick said most of the Pinecones would make it. That means some probably won't . . . and guess who will be the one who doesn't."

"I think Lauren's right," said Ashley. "In other gymnastics schools they have tests, and you each move up at your own pace."

"Shut up, Ashley," I said.

Ashley put her hands on her hips. "You can't tell me to shut up, and I'm taking a shower. Because Becky's right; with boys in the gym we should be clean."

Ashley stepped into the shower. "She belongs in Becky's group," I muttered.

"Patrick would never split us up," argued Jodi. "He'd never do it."

"Right," I said. But I had a sickening feeling in the bottom of my stomach.

"Oh, yeah?" said Lauren. "Just ask him."

Darlene looked at me. "Maybe you should go ask Patrick exactly what he meant," she said.

"Me? You're the captain," I said.

Darlene squared her shoulders. "You're right. Maybe you and I should go together."

"Well, I already know the answer," said Lauren. "It's a test to see who's going to move up. Patrick made it perfectly clear. I don't want to talk to him about it."

Darlene and I looked at each other. "I think we have to find out exactly what's going on, don't you?" she said.

I nodded my head.

"I'm going home," said Lauren.

"Wait for me," I urged her.

Lauren shook her head. "I've got a ton of homework," she said. I stared at her. Lauren and I go to the same school, and *I* didn't have a ton of homework. Lauren's a better student than I am. She's in the "gifted and talented" program, and I'm not, but I still knew she was just making up an excuse.

"Come on. Darlene and I will be just a minute," I said.

"No," said Lauren, zipping her gym bag shut. "I'm going. I'll see you tomorrow."

I grabbed Lauren's arm. Somehow I just didn't want her to go. "It's okay, Cindi," she said softly. "I'm not quitting. I just want to go home."

"But Patrick won't split up the Pinecones," I said.

Lauren just shook her head sadly. "Ashley's right. You haven't been listening to him. Remember the shark." Then Lauren walked out of the locker room and out the door.

11

"Maybe" Is Not
a Comforting Thought

I had to find Patrick and get the truth. Patrick was nowhere to be seen in the gym. The boys were just coming out from around the screens. Jared looked red in the face. Darlene waved to him, and he could barely lift his hand to wave back.

"Where's Patrick?" I asked Jodi's mom.

"I think he's in his office," said Sarah. She smiled at me. "Cindi, your brother's got a lot of gumption."

"Thanks," I said. "Do you mean he didn't fall off the rings?"

"I mean he wasn't afraid to try anything," said Jodi's mom.

Jared sat down on the bench and toweled himself off. He raised his eyebrows. "She's tough," he whispered to me.

"Welcome to gymnastics, bro," I said.

We walked up the stairs to Patrick's office. I knocked on his door.

Patrick looked up from some charts that he was entering into his computer. "Hi, Cindi, Darlene," he said. "What can I do for you . . . whoops! I should amend that for Cindi. What can I do for you *besides* getting rid of the boys in the gym?"

"It doesn't have anything to do with boys," I said.

Patrick smiled at me. "Good. So what's bothering you?" he asked.

"You said that this was a test to see if we could go to the next level, but say, for example, that Darlene can do it, and I can't."

Patrick shook his head. "Cindi, I've got every confidence that you can do it. To be honest, of all the Pinecones I've got the most confidence in you and Darlene."

"Uh, thanks, Patrick, but that's not the point. I mean, the Pinecones have been together from the beginning. If you give a test and one of us doesn't pass it, what happens to that person?"

Patrick pulled on his earlobe and put his fingers through his hair. I guess all of us have nervous tics.

"Cindi, that's the hard thing about all sports. We can't stay at the same level, and we make good friends no matter what team we're on."

"Wait a minute, Patrick," argued Darlene. "We're not like my dad's team. You can't just trade us like we're football players or something."

"Of course not," said Patrick. "Look, I love the way you girls have pulled together as a team, but some of you are bound to improve faster than others. I can't hold you back just because you want to stick together."

"Fine, put Ashley in a new group and keep the rest of us," I said.

Patrick laughed as if I were kidding, but I wasn't.

"Cindi, the test isn't for a couple of weeks. I've never asked the impossible of you girls, and I'm not doing so now."

"Yeah, but this is a very hard move. What if we can't do it without a spot?"

"I'll be in position to help anyone who needs it," said Patrick. "It's not going to be like a meet where I have to get out of the way."

"Yeah, but suppose one of us still can't do it."

"I'll give each girl two chances. Look, if some of you move up and some don't, it won't be the end of the world. Everybody will still be coming to the same gym. You'll be working out in the same place. Besides, you haven't considered one thing."

"What's that?" I asked.

"It's possible that all the Pinecones will make it. In fact, that's what I'm hoping."

"But if we *don't*?" I argued. My voice was cracking like Jared's.

"Change is a fact of life that all athletes have to live with," said Patrick. "It's why I keep using the shark analogy. You can't stay still and stay alive."

"But sharks kill people. Splitting us up might kill the Pinecones."

Patrick sighed. "Cindi, I've got to look at the big picture."

I hate it when adults start talking like that. Patrick might be one of my favorite adults in the whole world, but he was wrong about this. No "big picture" was worth splitting up the Pinecones.

"Seriously, Patrick," I said, "I don't think this test is a good idea."

"Cindi, I told you. I'm not worried about you."

"Come on, Cindi," said Darlene. "Stop beating a dead horse. We've got lots of time before the test. Think about what Patrick said. Maybe we'll all make it."

"Maybe" is not a very comforting thought.

12

You're Just a Dope, That's All

Jared and Ryan were waiting for me. The rest of the guys were laughing and joking, but Jared stood a little bit to the side. He looked a little sad. I wondered if anything was wrong.

Tim was supposed to pick us up, but he wasn't there yet. Lauren came out. I guess she hadn't left as quickly as she had said.

"Did you find out anything?" she asked. "I couldn't leave without finding out what Patrick said."

"Uh, Patrick thinks we're all going to make it," I said honestly. I couldn't bear to tell Lauren that Patrick hadn't promised not to split up the Pinecones if we all didn't make it.

"Please ride home with us," I urged her.

"I need to walk," she said.

"Lauren," I begged. Lauren looked at me and shrugged. Then she gave me a halfhearted smile. "I guess I *am* being a dope, huh? Okay, I'll take a ride, but no talk about the test, promise?"

"I promise," I said.

Just then Becky came out of the gym. "Hi, Cindi," she said, "Hi, Lauren," giving us a big smile. I turned around. Becky doesn't usually act so friendly unless she wants something. She put her gym bag down as if she were staying to chat.

"What do you want, Becky?" I asked her.

"Uh, nothing," said Becky, as she kept glancing over her shoulder at the boys. I sighed. You don't grow up with four older brothers without sensing when girls are being friendly to you because of them. Even when I was little, I hated it when my older brothers' girlfriends would pretend to want to play dolls with me, just so my brothers would think they were cute.

I didn't find Becky cute.

Ryan broke away from the other boys and came over to Becky, Lauren, and me.

"Cindi!" he exclaimed as if we hadn't seen each other for a long time. He was sounding as phony as Becky.

"I got my invitation and RSVP-ed," he said. "Jared doesn't suspect a thing."

"You can't talk about it now," I whispered.

"What invitation?" asked Becky innocently.

"We're having a surprise party for Jared," said Ryan. I could have strangled him.

"We?" I muttered under my breath — so far Ryan hadn't done any of the work.

"It's going to be great," said Ryan, ignoring me.

Becky turned her icy blue eyes on me. She tried to make them look big and innocent. Fat chance.

"It sounds neat," she said. "I wish I could come. When is it?"

"It's on the fifteenth," said Ryan.

"Oh, the day of our big test. . . ."

"Your group is having a test, too?" asked Lauren. "I didn't realize it."

"At least if Becky moves up, and we all pass we won't be in her group," I hissed.

"What are you whispering about?" demanded Becky.

I felt myself blushing. As much as I don't like Becky, I shouldn't have whispered about her in front of Ryan.

"Uh . . . uh. . . ." I stammered.

"Becky can come to the party, can't she?" Ryan asked. "And I was going to ask you to invite the other guys from gymnastics. It'd be fun if they all came. Some of these guys are neat."

"It's too late to send them an invitation," I whispered. "Just tell them about it, okay?"

Ryan winked at me. "Okeydokey! We can tell Becky right now."

"Thanks," said Becky cheerfully.

Lauren and I exchanged glances. I shrugged my shoulders. Becky was so pushy it was almost pathetic.

Just then Tim drove up. Becky and Ryan started babbling about the party. Jared broke away from the other guys. "Shh," I warned.

" 'Bye, Ryan," cooed Becky, as if she were nine years old, instead of thirteen.

She bumped into Jared as he was coming toward us and started to giggle. Jared stared at her as if she were nuts.

Jared climbed into the front seat. "What were you all laughing about with Becky?" he asked.

I gulped. I'm a terrible liar. I couldn't think of anything to say. I nudged Ryan with my elbow, hoping he would come up with something.

"Uh, Cindi and Lauren just told Becky and me a stupid gymnastics joke," said Ryan. "What season is it when you're on a trampoline?"

"Who cares?" asked Jared. He sounded as if he was in a lousy mood.

"Springtime," said Tim.

"You got it!" shouted Ryan, practically deafening me. *He* certainly was in a terrific mood.

"Ryan, it sounds like you're having a good time, even with a woman coach," said Tim.

"Yeah, when I started I didn't realize how good our coach would be. She's awesome."

"She's good, but the moves are so hard," complained Jared.

I grinned. I loved it. Ryan actually liked having a woman coach, and my own brother was admitting that gymnastics was difficult. In fact, he was sounding downright dejected.

I decided I had to give Ryan credit. "I'm glad you guys like it. I guess in a couple of months, I'll be going to your meets."

"I probably won't even make the team," groused Jared. "Take vaulting. I can't believe how hard it is. It looks easy, but when I run onto the board nothing happens."

"It takes a while to get the rhythm going to get on a springboard," I said. "You have to hit it just right."

"I hit it and go nowhere," said Jared.

"You gotta just keep trying," I said.

"That's what Sarah says," said Jared. "She keeps counting the steps off for me."

"That's the only way to learn," I said.

"I think it just comes natural to me," bragged Ryan. I gave him a dirty look. Maybe I had been too quick to give him credit. We dropped Ryan off at his house.

"Well, he certainly seems to be enjoying himself," said Tim.

"Why not?" said Jared with a sigh. "He's learning everything so quickly. I can't believe how easy this stuff looks when someone else does it, and how hard it really is!"

"Tell me about it," I laughed. I thought about all the years that I had been the only one doing gymnastics in my family, and everybody thought a back flip was *sooo* easy.

I smiled at Jared. "You know, brother, I actually feel sorry for you. But you'll get it. You just have to keep doing it."

"Easy for *you* to say," muttered Jared. "I've been watching you. You're really good."

"Thanks," I said.

Tim laughed as we pulled up in Lauren's driveway. "I can't believe it. Lauren, you and I are witnessing a miracle. Cindi and Jared aren't fighting, and they're actually complimenting each other."

"Well, it's true, Tim," said Jared. "Cindi's terrific. I didn't realize it until I started watching her every day. Cindi's almost as good as Becky, and Becky's the best in the gym. Don't you agree, Lauren?"

Lauren started to get out of the car. "Uh, yeah . . . Cindi's really good. She probably doesn't belong in the Pinecones anymore."

"Lauren . . ." I protested. Lauren shut the door. She didn't exactly slam it, but I knew she was upset.

"You dope!" I yelled at Jared.

"What did I say wrong?" he protested.

I rested my head against the window of the backseat as I looked up at Lauren going into her house.

"Nothing. You're just a dope, that's all," I grumbled.

Jared looked hurt, but I didn't care. Maybe he hadn't meant to hurt Lauren's feelings, but I knew that she was hurting. I just didn't know what I could do about it.

13

Every Change
Isn't for the Worse

There were only a few days left before the test. Almost every day we practiced the new move.

"Darlene's got it!" whispered Ashley to me as we watched Darlene slowly lower herself from her handstand to the reverse press on the beam.

"Beam has always been Darlene's strongest event," said Jodi. She twirled a lock of her long blonde hair. Jodi looked nervous. "I can't believe we're having this stupid test so soon," she said. "I've never done it without Patrick spotting me."

"He said he'll be ready to spot us when we do it for the test."

Jodi gave me a disgusted look. "Right, and if he does spot us, we haven't really done the trick."

"Even with Patrick's spot, I haven't come close," groaned Lauren.

"Don't worry," said Ti An. "I only did it a couple of times without a spot. It's really hard."

"Ti An," said Lauren with a sigh, "please stop trying to make me feel better."

Patrick waved to Jodi to come and try it.

"I did it yesterday without a spot," bragged Ashley.

"Good for you," I said sarcastically. But Ashley didn't get the sarcasm.

I wrinkled my nose. Jodi hit the board off-balance and couldn't hold the handstand. She dropped off the beam to try again. But the second time she overshot the beam and Patrick had to grab her legs to help her into the handstand. Once she got steadied she was strong enough to lower her hips into the reverse press.

It was Lauren's turn. I really wanted Lauren to make it. I knew she needed a shot of confidence. Lauren and I are so close that sometimes I believe if I just wish her to do well she will.

I watched as she ran for the board, but Ashley spoiled my concentration. "I think I've really got it mastered now," chirped Ashley. "Probably you, me, Ti An, and now maybe Darlene are going to be the only ones to move up," she said.

I whirled around to glare at her. "Ashley, put

a gag in it. Don't you ever say anything like that again."

"What's your problem?" whined Ashley. "I was only giving you and me a compliment. I'm just being realistic."

"Being realistic is overrated," I muttered.

"Is that a joke?" asked Ti An.

"No," I said. Lauren was flopped on the beam like a beached whale. "What happened?" I asked Ti An.

"She couldn't hold the press," said Ti An. "She kind of fell over like a piece of baloney."

Ashley giggled.

I glared at her again. "It was Ti An who said Lauren looked like baloney, not me," protested Ashley.

"Sorry, Cindi," said Ti An.

"It's not your fault," I said. I knew Ti An didn't have a mean bone in her. I couldn't say as much for Ashley.

"Cindi, it's your turn," called out Patrick. "You'll do it with no mistakes," whispered Lauren to me as we passed each other. But it sounded more like a curse than wishing me luck.

"Okay, Cindi," said Patrick, smiling at me. "Remember, the key is control."

I took a deep breath before I began my run. I ran fast for the board, but I could feel that I was

84

running a little flat-footed. I must have miscounted my approach because I hit the board all wrong. Instead of springing into the air, I went up with my hips bent. I reached out for the beam, but I didn't have enough height for my handstand. I slipped under the beam.

Patrick shook his head. "Remember, the idea is *on* the beam, not under it."

"Thank you for that good advice," I said. I had meant it as a joke, but I must have sounded pretty sarcastic.

"Cindi, relax," said Patrick. "You've done this before. You'll do it this next time. Concentrate."

I went to start my run again. I remembered to salute Patrick. I ran for the board and reached out for the beam, but this time I had too much height. I came down hard on my wrist.

"Ouch!" I yelled as my left hand gave out beneath me. I fell hard onto the beam and then tumbled to the floor.

Suddenly, from between the screens, Jared came running over to me.

He got to me even before Patrick could get there. "Cindi, are you okay?" he asked.

Patrick knelt beside me. I wiggled my wrist. It wasn't broken, or even badly sprained. "What are you doing over here?" I asked Jared. I was annoyed. It was bad enough that I had fallen. I didn't need Jared hovering over me like a mother hen.

"Uh . . . I was watching through the screens, and I saw you fall. . . ." Jared stammered.

Patrick stood up. "Jared, the divider is there so that you can concentrate on your *own* gymnastics, not on Cindi's."

"Sorry," said Jared.

"You've got to learn that Cindi can take care of herself. She's taken lots of falls in gymnastics, and so will you. But leave the worrying up to the coaches. You should stay with your group and Sarah. Now go back to your team."

Jared had turned a bright red. Now I knew what *I* look like when I get embarrassed. He slunk back behind the screen.

I held my left wrist in my right hand. Maybe I did sprain it. "Is it okay?" Patrick asked me.

"It hurts," I admitted.

"Go put ice on it," said Patrick.

I stared at him. "I can't. It's in the boys' locker room, remember?"

Patrick frowned. I had to admit I felt a little bit of satisfaction that Patrick had forgotten what a pain in the neck the boys' locker room had become.

"Girls, I'm going with Cindi to get ice for her wrist," said Patrick, looking at his watch. "It's

86

almost time to finish up. Lauren, lead the team in some conditioning. Let's say thirty sit-ups and twenty push-ups."

The Pinecones groaned in unison.

"Why me?" asked Lauren.

"Because I asked you," said Patrick.

Patrick and I walked to what I still thought of as the parents' lounge. Patrick poked his head halfway in the door.

"It's empty," he said. "You can come in with me."

We walked into the boys' locker room. The comfy couches had been pushed together and rows of hooks lined one wall. There were clothes and shoes strewn all over the place.

"I'll have to post some rules around here," said Patrick.

Patrick got me some ice from the ice machine. "Boys are really messier than girls," I said as I looked around. "It was a big mistake to let boys in the gym. Everything's been rotten since they started coming here."

Patrick wrapped the ice in a towel and put it on my wrist. "The new boys' locker room will be finished soon," he said. "They'll be out of here."

"It'll never be the same," I warned him. "You'll have to defumigate this room before you dare let the parents back in."

Patrick gave me a half smile. "Somehow, Cindi, I don't think it's the boys' locker room that's upsetting you so much these past couple of weeks."

Patrick guided me over to one of the couches. "I've been looking for a chance to talk to you alone, Cindi." Patrick paused. He flopped down on one of the couches. I looked at him. I wondered if Patrick was mad at me because I had been so negative about the boys.

But he surprised me. "You're not helping Lauren by fouling up," he said finally.

"I'm not messing up on purpose," I protested.

"I believe you," said Patrick. "But subconsciously you don't want to do well because you're worried about Lauren."

"I don't know what you're talking about," I lied. I was too flustered to admit how close Patrick had come to the truth.

Patrick was too smart for me. "Cindi, you know what I'm talking about."

"I do not," I said. "My bad mood lately has nothing to do with Lauren and the test. It's just that the chemistry of the gym has changed because of the boys. You can smell it." I held my nose.

Patrick shook his head. "Cindi, the boys are just a smokescreen. You're not worried about the test for yourself but for Lauren. Cindi, you're a competitor. There's an engine inside you. You can't shut it down and think you're helping anyone."

I frowned. Half of me liked what Patrick was saying. I loved the idea that he called me a competitor. I knew Patrick well enough to know that was high praise. But half of me still liked it better when I could just blame my lousy mood on the boys and Jared.

"Why can't things stay the same?" I was practically wailing. "Why do things have to change?"

"Cindi, you can't stop time."

I glared at Patrick. "Please don't call me a shark. I hate that shark motto."

"I'm beginning to wish I had never said it myself," admitted Patrick. "But I am right about not stopping time. And, Cindi, I'm right about who you are. I never worry about you in a meet. You always find a way to rise to the occasion. It's almost as if you were born to compete. The team is fired up by your competitiveness. That's not a bad thing. All great teams have to have what we call 'a gamer.' But you can't hide that competitive nature. You can't pretend to be something you're not. Your job is to be an example to the others, not to foul up so that they'll feel better."

"But, Patrick . . . this isn't a meet. I'm competing against my friends. What if I make it and Lauren doesn't?"

Patrick just looked at me. "Aren't you selling Lauren a little short?" he asked me.

I swallowed hard. Patrick had a point. He stood up and took a look around the "locker room." "You were right about one thing," he said.

"What's that?" I asked.

"It was a mistake to put the boys in here. This *is* the most comfortable room in the gym. I can't wait till we get it back."

"I still say it'll never be the same," I warned him.

"Things never are," said Patrick.

"That's what I hate," I said.

Patrick held the door open for me. "Every change isn't for the worse," he said to me.

If only I could believe him. . . .

14

Put-Down Artist

I went back to the Pinecones feeling a lot calmer, which is more than I can say for the atmosphere in the girls' locker room.

Becky had her hands on her hips and was staring down at Gloria, one of the girls in the more advanced group. "Well of course, I'm planning on passing the test so that I can become an elite gymnast. What else is the point?" Gloria and Becky continued their argument as they went into the shower.

"What's going on?" I whispered to Darlene.

"The advanced group is having a test next week, too," said Darlene. "Gloria's mad at Becky because Becky isn't worried about it and Gloria is."

Jodi came up to my other side. She was giggling. "Wouldn't it be great if Becky were overconfident?" she whispered. "I'd love to see her fail."

"Don't hope for that," I warned her. "If we all move up a level, and she doesn't, we'll be in her group."

"I never thought of it that way," said Jodi. "Who would have thought I'd be in a position to have to root for Becky?"

"I wish everybody would just shut up about the test," griped Lauren. "Maybe you all have a problem with joining Becky's group, but it's not my problem. I'm not going anywhere. I'll be the oldest living Pinecone. Someday they'll probably plant me in Estes National Park, and tourist buses will stop to look at me."

Jodi started laughing. It wasn't really funny. Lauren always finds it easy to get laughs just by putting herself down.

Lauren was on a roll, and she couldn't stop. "It's a proven fact that I'm not going anywhere in gymnastics. It's some kind of punishment. I was never nice enough to the kids who didn't do well at school when I kept being put in faster groups. It's a proven fact that nobody's good at everything. Like water, I've found my level."

Ti An giggled nervously.

"Lauren, cut it out," I urged her.

"And," continued Lauren, "it's a proven fact that my best friend, Cindi Jockett, is going to give me another lecture on 'not giving up.' " Lauren glared at me. "Let's just change the subject. No more talk about the test."

I was bright red now, but it wasn't from embarrassment. Lauren was making me mad with her defeatist attitude.

Before I could answer her, Darlene stepped in to try to lighten things up. "Come on, you two. You're making the Pinecones look like Becky's group."

"Maybe we won't be the Pinecones for long," said Lauren.

"I thought you said you wanted to change the subject," said Darlene, sounding exasperated.

"I do," admitted Lauren.

"Good," said Darlene. "Cindi, I've been thinking. Have you figured a way to get Jared out of the house while everybody comes over for the surprise?"

"No," I admitted. I had been so preoccupied with our big test that I had almost forgotten about Jared's surprise party.

"Well, I've got a great idea," said Darlene. "The party's planned for five-thirty. Jared's got gymnastics till five, so if you let him go home, he might run into some of the guests. But that's the day of our big test, remember?"

"How could any of us forget?" said Lauren.

"Why don't you tell Jared that we think he'll bring us luck?" asked Darlene. "We'll tell him we want him to stay and cheer for us."

I started to guffaw. "Jared? Good luck?"

"Wait a minute," said Jodi. "We've won lots of meets when Jared's been cheering for us."

"The point is to keep an eye on Jared until the party. We'll tell him we think that we'll pass if he sticks around. Then we can go over to your house with Jared, and he won't suspect a thing."

"That's a great idea!" said Jodi.

"But what if . . ." I started to blurt out. I shut my mouth. I was about to say, "What if Lauren doesn't pass, and she's not a Pinecone anymore, and we'll all be in a lousy mood?" I shut my mouth quickly.

"What if . . . what?" Lauren asked suspiciously. I knew she suspected that I didn't think she would pass the test.

"Nothing," I said quickly. "It's a great idea."

When we got out of the locker room, Jared and the other boys were just leaving.

Darlene walked up and asked Jared to wait. You could tell he loved the idea that she had singled him out.

He loved even more the idea that he was going to be our good luck charm.

"Of course I'll stay and watch the test until it's over," he said.

I almost choked because he sounded so pleased to be asked. Ryan begged to be able to stay, too. "I'll be even more good luck," he said.

"I doubt it," I said to him. I took him aside and whispered to him that it was a plan to keep Jared away from the house while the other guests had a chance to hide downstairs.

Ryan gave me a huge wink that I'm sure Jared could see. "I'll keep cool," he whispered.

I gave him a dirty look. Ryan just grinned at me. "Seriously, Cindi, maybe I will bring you luck."

"You're really loving gymnastics, aren't you?" I asked him.

Ryan nodded. He seemed almost shy.

"Well, make sure you don't let Jared know what's going on," I warned him.

"Don't worry," said Ryan. "My lips are sealed."

15

What if My Best Isn't Good Enough?

Finally it was the morning of the test, and I was *so* nervous. I couldn't remember being this nervous, even before a big meet. Mom and Dad sensed that I was on pins and needles, but they thought it was just because of the suspense of Jared's surprise party.

Dad rubbed his hands together when he came down to breakfast. "Where's Jared?" he whispered.

"Still getting dressed," I said.

"I've got to congratulate you, Cindi," said Dad. "I think you really kept a secret this time."

"I had help," I said. "The Pinecones would have murdered me if I had given it away." Then I

looked down at my cereal bowl. "The Pinecones."
I was so used to thinking of us as a team. What
would happen if by the end of the day we weren't
one? Patrick could talk all he wanted to about
not being able to stop time, but it didn't make
me feel any better. I wanted there always to be
"The Pinecones," and I always wanted to be one.
What was so bad about that?

Jared came clumping down the stairs, late as
usual. He was wearing an Evergreen Gymnastics
Academy T-shirt. It was brand new, and I could
tell that it was an extra-large. Jared loves to wear
his T-shirts big. Maybe if he does enough gymnastics he'll finally grow the muscles to fit them.

"I didn't know Patrick had given you T-shirts
yet," I said.

"Sarah gave them to us," said Jared. "She said
she had them made up special in large sizes as
soon as she heard she was going to coach the
boys' team."

"Shouldn't you be saving it for your first
meet?" asked Dad. "I remember when Cindi wore
her first Evergreen leotard."

"Today's an important day," said Jared. Jared
winked at me.

Dad practically choked on his muffin. He
looked at me. I knew he thought that Jared was
talking about his surprise party.

"You okay, Dad?" asked Jared.

"Jared's talking about the Pinecones' test today," I told Dad. "You've been away. Patrick is testing us on a strength move on the beam today. Those of us who can do it are going to move up to the next level."

"Our coach wants us to watch all the testing," said Jared. "She says we can learn a lot watching you girls work under pressure. I sure hope you all make it. I don't want anybody splitting up the Pinecones. I owe a lot to the Pinecones."

"You do?" I exclaimed. Did Jared know that the Pinecones had done most of the work for his party?

"Yeah," said Jared, "I would never be in gymnastics if it weren't for you and the Pinecones. Besides, think how awful it would be if you moved up and Becky failed and you had to work out with Becky every day. I'd like to see Becky fail."

Now it was my turn to practically choke on my breakfast. "I thought you *liked* Becky," I exclaimed.

"She's a dork," said Jared. "I hate girls who pretend to be stupid. She could beat me at any gymnastics event with one hand tied behind her, and yet she pretends to be so helpless. *Yuk.*"

"She — " I clapped my hand over my mouth. I had been about to say, "She's coming to your party." Here I had finally kept a secret, and I was about to ruin it all.

"She what?" asked Jared.

"Uh . . . she seems to like Ryan," I said. When in trouble, gossip. Jared loved gossip. "And Ryan seems to like her," I added.

"Well, Ryan's not very smart when it comes to girls," said Jared.

Mom and Dad practically convulsed on the floor, they were laughing so hard, but I had to hand it to my brother. He's pretty smart, and he can be nice. I thought about him running over to me when I fell. I was annoyed at him at the time, but it showed he cared.

After school, Jared wished me luck as we separated for the locker rooms.

I don't know what it was like over in the boys' locker room, but over in the girls' it was tense. When we're nervous because of a big meet, there's a certain excitement in the gym. It must be the way rock stars feel right before they go onstage.

Today didn't have that atmosphere. Mostly I think there was just fear. Fear and excitement are an okay combination, but fear without excitement stinks. It affected everybody . . . everybody who was human, that is. Becky was perfectly cool.

"I'm so excited about the party this afternoon," she said. "Just as soon as my group finishes our test, I'm going to get ready. I'm sure we'll all pass."

"So will the Pinecones," I said, pulling on a clean T-shirt. "You'd better watch it, Becky. The Pinecones will be moving up on you."

"Maybe *some* of you," taunted Becky.

"All of us. We're going to stick together."

"Yeah," joked Jodi, who was standing next to Lauren, "maybe we'll all flunk and stay together." Lauren laughed, but she sounded jittery.

I whirled around to face Jodi and Lauren. "No, we're all gonna do our best." I thought about what Patrick had told me, about how I was the competitor. "The team is fired up by your competitiveness," Patrick had said to me. But we weren't competing against another team. Now it was just us against ourselves, but I hated my team being so negative. We almost wanted to do badly on the test because that way we'd stay together. It would feel awful to remain together that way. Maybe that's what Patrick meant when he said that I couldn't hold back time.

"Listen to me," I said. "All of us are strong

enough to pass this test. All we have to do is just do it."

"Oh, goody," said Becky. "Just what the Pinecones need, backbone medicine."

"The Pinecones don't need medicine. We started together. We're going to move up together."

"You can't guarantee that," said Becky.

"Oh, no?" I said. "Just watch us. And you'd better start worrying about yourself, Becky. Maybe you'll end up lower than a Pinecone."

Becky glowered at me. I don't think the idea of not passing her test had ever occurred to her.

Darlene gave me a high five. "That's telling her," she said.

"It's not her I'm worried about," I whispered. Jodi and Lauren were getting dressed excruciatingly slowly as if they really wanted to hold back time.

"Come on, Lauren," I said impatiently. "Let's go."

"We'll be there," said Lauren. "You don't have to wait for us."

"We're going out together," I said.

Lauren put on a leotard. "Cindi," she whined, "it's a proven fact that I don't mind being left behind. Go, if you're in such a hurry."

I sat down on the bench. "Cut out the 'proven

fact,' " I said. "You're not going to be left behind."

"It was a great pep talk you gave in front of Becky," said Lauren. "But you and I have got to be honest with each other."

"Lauren, I'm telling the truth. You *are* going to pass the test."

"You can't do it for me," said Lauren softly. She didn't sound angry. She didn't sound whiny. She just sounded honest.

Her words made me want to cry. "Trust me," I said. "Just do your best."

"Yeah," said Lauren. "But what if my best isn't good enough?"

16

Retire
the Shark Motto

We warmed up while Becky's group was doing their testing on the uneven bars.

We were supposed to be concentrating on our own warm-up, but when I heard a gasp go up, I couldn't help but look. The bars depend on upper body strength and a sense of rhythm. Becky was so strong. She did a backward hip circle to a handstand, which totally depends on the strength of the grip of your hands and your shoulder muscles. She made it look easy. Then she did a handstand dismount with a one-quarter turn. Again, it's a move that depends on an incredibly strong grip because you have to shift your weight first from one hand to another.

I heard a burst of applause. The boys and Jodi's mom had finished their workout and were watching. They were certainly impressed. I couldn't blame them. I was pretty impressed myself.

"At least you won't have to worry about moving up to her group," Lauren whispered to me. "She's almost in a class by herself around here."

"*You* don't have to worry about her, either," I said.

"I never did," said Lauren.

"Lauren, please," I begged. "What can I say to make you stop being so negative?"

Lauren shrugged her shoulders. I felt so helpless. There had to be something I could say to make it easier for her, but all the words in the world didn't seem to be doing much good.

Patrick blew on his whistle. "All right. The advanced group has finished their testing. Let's have the Pinecones come over to the beam."

Lauren sighed next to me. I couldn't think of anything to say, so I just took her hand and led her over to the beam.

Patrick smiled at us. "I know you girls are nervous, but please remember this is just for your own good."

"Patrick," complained Jodi. "All adults say

that. I thought you'd never sink so low."

Patrick laughed. "You're right, Jodi. I'm sorry. I know this is tough on all of you. Jodi, why don't you go first."

"Why me?" asked Jodi.

"Because then you'll get it over with," he said. Patrick took his position, ready to spot Jodi if she needed it.

Jodi took a deep breath. I was worried that she would overshoot the beam, but she didn't. She pulled into her handstand beautifully. Then, very slowly, she lowered her legs and rotated them in front of her until she was pressing down with her hands. She held it for fifteen seconds.

Patrick wrote on his clipboard, but he had a pleased look on his face.

Jodi's face was flushed.

She hopped off the beam. "You did it!" I cheered her and gave her a low five.

Ti An went next. The handstand-reverse press seemed to be just made for Ti An. There are moves that are hard for everybody else to do, but fit one person like a glove. Ti An performed the move so smoothly, she could have been demonstrating it on television.

Darlene was next. I heard Jared yell from the benches, "Go, Pinecones!"

Darlene wobbled a little getting into her handstand, but she didn't have any trouble lowering herself into the reverse press.

"That's the way, Pinecones!" shouted Jared. Jared even cheered for Ashley. Ashley slipped on her first try getting into her handstand, but she did it on the second try.

"Patrick said it didn't matter that I messed up the first time," chirped Ashley, as she came back to our bench. "He said I've really gained in upper body strength since I've become a Pinecone. I loved it when the boys cheered for me. It made me feel like it was a meet."

Lauren bit on her thumbnail. "It's *not* a meet," she said. "Jared doesn't have to keep yelling for the Pinecones."

"He's only trying to help," I said.

"Well, I don't want him yelling when I'm doing it," Lauren said. "I hope Patrick picks me soon. The suspense is killing me."

Patrick blew his whistle.

"Cindi, you're next," he said, looking down at his clipboard.

"Good luck," said Lauren. I looked at her. When you've been friends with someone since kindergarten, you know all their different voices. I could tell Lauren meant it when she wished me good luck.

"Thanks," I said.

I walked up to Patrick and whispered to him, "Lauren needs to go before me. I can go last."

Patrick shook his head. "Cindi, I'm the coach. Let me do my job. Your job is to do the handstand mount to the reverse press."

"Go for it, Sis," yelled Jared.

I blinked.

I walked to the edge of the approach mat for my run to the beam. I wiggled my head back and forth, trying to loosen the tension in my neck. I closed my eyes for a second. I blocked out the sound of the boys cheering on the bench. I blocked out my fear that Lauren wouldn't make it. I couldn't think about her now. I had to do it myself.

I ran for the springboard. It gave a satisfying *brong!* sound when I landed. I controlled my jump into the air, reaching for the beam and bending my hips over the center of the beam so that I would have more control. I pushed my way up to a handstand. It took all my strength. All those months of push-ups and conditioning with Patrick were finally paying off.

I held the handstand for a beat, then opened my legs into a straddle and bent my hips again, slowly lowering my weight over my hands. I lifted my chest so that I was in a perfect press. Patrick checked his stopwatch.

He gave me a thumbs up and I relaxed my aching arms and rested on the beam.

"Beautiful, Cindi," said Patrick.

I hopped off the beam. Jodi handed me a towel to dry off.

"Lauren," said Patrick. Lauren looked at the ground as she walked toward the approach.

I crossed my fingers on both hands. Then I quickly uncrossed them. I had read in a book somewhere that crossing fingers on both hands was bad luck.

Lauren took a deep breath. She ran for the springboard. I think she hit it a little off balance because it gave a weak *brong!* sound, but she had enough height to reach out for the beam. She pushed her hips over the beam. I could see her arms wobbling as she struggled to control her legs into her handstand.

I was scared Lauren was going to fall off the beam, but she didn't. Now she just had to rotate her hips into the reverse press.

I could see the sweat on Lauren's face as she fought to keep control. Her arms were really shaking.

Patrick looked down at his stopwatch. I was holding my breath, counting in my head. "Nine . . . ten . . . eleven . . ." I could see Lauren's shoulders shaking. I knew she couldn't hold it much longer. Just three more seconds . . . that's all she needed. "Twelve . . . thirteen . . . fourteen . . . fifteen!"

Lauren collapsed belly-down on the beam. Slowly, she rolled off and tumbled down onto the mats. She lay on her back, breathing hard. Then she rolled over onto all fours and crawled over to the rest of us.

I clapped her on the back, "Careful," she said. "I think I'm gonna ache all over for a week."

"But you did it," I exclaimed.

Lauren grinned at me. "I did, didn't I?" she said. She took a deep breath. "Well, you were a great inspiration."

I did a double take. For a second, I thought she was being sarcastic.

"I wanted you to do it," I said.

"Hey, Cindi, I mean it," said Lauren. "I saw how strong you were, and I thought, hey, wait a minute. I've been doing the same conditioning as Cindi. I'm strong, too. After watching you, I just made up my mind that I was gonna do it."

Patrick looked up from his chart. He was beaming. "Congratulations, Pinecones," he said. "I was almost sure this would be the outcome. You all made it. I knew you were improving, but this clinches it. The Pinecones will move up together as a group. Everybody relax and have a great weekend."

"You're not going to change our name, are you?" I asked Patrick.

Patrick shook his head. "I'm not that foolish," he said. "That's the first thing I learned when I became a coach — 'if it ain't broke, don't fix it.' "

"That's ungrammatical," said Lauren.

"Who cares?" I said. "I like that as a motto a lot better than that stuff about dead sharks."

Patrick grinned. "It's live sharks, remember?" he said. "But I think you're right. I'll retire the shark motto."

I turned to go. "Cindi," whispered Patrick. "Have a good time tonight." I had forgotten that Patrick knew all about our surprise party. "You deserve a celebration," he said.

"I didn't do anything special," I protested.

"You did your best when you were tempted not to," he said. "That's special enough."

"When it came down to the wire, I couldn't help myself," I admitted. "Even if I had wanted to foul up for Lauren, I couldn't have."

Patrick nodded his head as if he understood. "That's what I like about you," he said.

17

Maybe Boys
in the Gym
Aren't So Bad

Jared and Ryan were waiting for us when we came out of the girls' locker room.

"The Pinecones are all coming over to our house to celebrate," I told Jared.

"Great. You were super, Cindi. I'm not kidding." Jared nudged me with his elbow. "Even Ryan was impressed."

Lauren started giggling behind me. I knew she was excited about the surprise party. "What's gotten into Lauren?" Jared asked suspiciously.

"Oh, she's just so excited she passed," I said. Darlene winked at me. I was worried. The Pinecones were being so obvious that I was sure Jared would suspect something.

I guess when it's still a week until your birthday your guard is down. Our house looked unnaturally quiet when we all walked up the driveway. Even Cleo didn't bark. I figured Mom and Dad must have had her downstairs with the other kids, waiting to surprise Jared.

We walked into the house. "Anybody home?" yelled Jared. Jared started to walk toward the kitchen.

"Where are you going?" I asked him.

"I'm starved," he said. "I'm getting something to eat."

"Naw, let's go downstairs to the rec room," I said. "I've got a move to show you that will really help your own gymnastics."

"Cindi, I'm sick of gymnastics, okay?" whined Jared. "I've been at the gym all afternoon. I watched all of you. I brought the Pinecones good luck. Now leave me alone."

I opened my mouth and shut it. I had to get Jared down to the rec room. I thought the hard part was going to be getting him to come home without running into any of his friends from school. But what if he just wouldn't go downstairs at all? I'd feel pretty silly yelling, "Surprise!" all by myself.

Luckily Darlene came to my rescue. "Come on, Jared," she said. "If you want to be good at gymnastics, you've got to think like a Pinecone."

If I had said something like that Jared would have laughed his head off, but instead he just gave Darlene a sheepish smile. "I'm not sure I want to go that far," he said, but he followed Darlene and the rest of us down the stairs.

The lights were out. I reached for the switch on the wall.

"SURPRISE!" yelled all his friends. Cleo started barking.

Jared literally turned white. You could see all the freckles stand out on his face. Then he kind of half ducked his head. Slowly he turned bright red.

"You . . . you . . ." he sputtered at me.

"Happy birthday!" I exclaimed. I gave him a hug. "Who says I can't keep a secret!"

The party was a great success. All of Jared's school friends were eager to meet the kids from gymnastics that they had been hearing about.

Mom and I were just about to go upstairs to get the cake when I heard Becky's high, simpering voice cut through the crowd. "Oh, Ryan," she tittered, "I couldn't arm wrestle with you. You're way too strong."

I rolled my eyes. "She's stronger than two Ryans put together," I said to my mother.

"Some girls are like that," said Mom.

"Well, okay, if you insist," twittered Becky. "But I know you'll win."

"Wait," I said to Mom, "I've got to see this."

"It's okay," said Mom. "Dad and I can bring down the cake."

I went over to the corner where Jared was clearing a space on a card table. "Ryan challenged Becky to an arm wrestling match," he explained.

"I heard," I said.

Becky pushed the hair out of her face and put her elbow on the table. She flexed her wrist. Ryan sat down on the opposite side. They started to arm wrestle. Becky pretended to be struggling. I could see the long muscle on her forearm tensing. She started to push Ryan's arm toward the table.

"Go, Becky!" I cheered.

Darlene looked startled. "Well, at least she's showing him that girls are stronger than boys," I said.

Ryan heard me. He grunted. Slowly Becky let Ryan raise his hand. Then suddenly the leverage changed, and Becky's arm flopped down on the table.

"Oh, Ryan . . . you're too strong for me."

"Give me a break," whispered Jared, standing next to me.

114

Ryan started to stand up and take a bow. "Hold it," I said. "I'll take you on."

Ryan laughed at me. "Don't be silly, Cindi. Becky's stronger than you, and I beat her."

"What's the matter?" I asked. "Afraid of a girl?"

Ryan's buddies all laughed. I sat down and put my elbow on the table.

Ryan sat back down. He grabbed my hand and tried to squeeze it, but I had all those calluses from the uneven bars. He couldn't hurt me.

Ryan caught me off guard and started to push my arm down. The back of my hand was just inches from the table. I tensed my bicep. Patrick had said I was a competitor. No way was I gonna let Ryan beat me.

Slowly I inched our hands back toward the center, then I began to push Ryan's arm down. Once I had the momentum, he really was no match for me. I gritted my teeth for one last push, and I pinned his wrist to the table.

"Yea, Cindi!" shouted the Pinecones. Jared was grinning at me. I stood up with my hands over my head and circled the room.

Jared was trying not to laugh too hard. Becky looked embarrassed.

"You shouldn't have let him win," I whispered to her as I drank in all the applause.

Becky looked mad enough to spit.

Lauren held out her hand. "Congratulations," she said. I couldn't stop grinning. Beating Ryan had been fun.

"Maybe boys in the gym are good for the Pinecones," Lauren said to me as we shook.

"I wouldn't go that far," I said. "They're still a lot of trouble."

Just then, Mom and Dad brought down Jared's cake. I looked around the room. Becky was still sulking. Jared and *all* the gymnasts were having a great time. Maybe Lauren was right. Maybe boys in the gym wasn't such a bad idea after all.

About the Author

Elizabeth Levy decided that the only way she could write about gymnastics was to try it herself. Besides taking classes she is involved with a group of young gymnasts near her home in New York City, and enjoys following their progress.

Elizabeth Levy's other Apple Paperbacks are *A Different Twist*, *The Computer That Said Steal Me*, and all the other books in THE GYMNASTS series.

She likes visiting schools to give talks and meet her readers. Kids love her presentation's opening. Why? "I start with a cartwheel!" says Levy. "At least I try to."

America's Favorite Series

THE BABY-SITTERS CLUB®

by Ann M. Martin

Collect Them All!

he seven girls at Stoneybrook Middle School get into
kinds of adventures...with school, boys, and, of course, baby-sitting!

For a complete listing of all the Baby-sitter Club titles write to :
Customer Service at the address below.
Available wherever you buy books...or use the coupon below.

APPLE®PAPERBACKS

Pick an Apple and Polish Off Some Great Reading!

NEW APPLE TITLES